LYN AND THE FUZZY

LYN AND THE FUZZY

Written and Illustrated by
JAMES RICE

PELICAN PUBLISHING COMPANY
GRETNA 1975

Library of Congress Cataloging in Publication Data

Rice, James, 1934—
   Lyn and the Fuzzy.
   SUMMARY: Grown from a special seed, Fuzzy, a huge,
strong, friendly creature, becomes Lyn's constant compan-
ion until the cold winds blow.

   1. Friendship—Fiction

   I. Title.

PZ7.R3634Ly   E   75-19096

ISBN 0–88289–087–5

Manufactured in the United States of America

Published by Pelican Publishing Company, Inc.
630 Burmaster Street, Gretna, Louisiana 70053

Designed by Gerald Bower

LYN AND THE FUZZY

Not so long ago in a place not
far from here lived a boy named
Lyn and a dog named Charley.
This is a story about Lyn, but it is hard
to talk about Lyn without mentioning Charley
because wherever you see one you are
likely to see the other.

Some days are fun and some days are
lazy and some days just pass and
are soon forgotten. Some days start
like other days, then turn into very
special days that are never forgotten.

Such a day happened to Lyn and
turned many days into very
special days.

Lyn liked to climb trees
and swing like a monkey way
up high, but today he
wanted to do something else.

It was fun to shoot baskets
with Zel and dribble back
and forth, but bounce and
throw and bounce and
throw—soon it's
just like
everything
else.

He stopped to play with Jason,
but Jason was too busy playing
with sow bugs to notice him.
Anyway, today he wasn't interested
in sow bugs.

It was fun to cut the grass
with Dad and watch the weeds
fall row after row, but not
today.

It was fun to watch Patti
count her dolls and play make-
believe. They often played
together, but today he wanted
something different to do.

It was fun to be in the
kitchen while Maria and Mom
were baking. There were
spicy, warm, sweet smells and
sticky bowls to lick, but sometimes
a boy needed something different
to do.

He walked outside alone
and stopped to look at some
soft, fuzzy dandelions moving
with every touch of the breeze.
They seemed almost alive. He lay
in the grass to watch the downy
petals quiver then float away—
now here, now gone.

Lyn wandered to a strange
pet shop.

The pets were unusual. They
did not seem very friendly.
The owner was stranger than
the pets as he bent to look
through thick smeared glasses
from behind the dusty counter.

Pets cost dollars, but little boys
have pennies.
"Ten dollars for a pet, ten cents for
a special fuzzy seed," said the
bent little old man.
—Fuzzy Seed?—
He continued, "Sprinkle lightly with
love, add a portion of trust, and
wrap it all in a dream, then
plant it deep while the sun is high
and warm.

"BUT BEWARE!
Beware the March
winds, and the cold winds
and the hot winds, and the
winds that blow and blow."

Lyn took the
seed and
sprinkled it
with love, covered it
with trust, and wrapped
it up tightly in a dream
then planted it in the woods
behind his house under the
sun, high and warm.

The grass grew and the flowers
bloomed. The fuzzy seed grew
into a large downy flower that
became soft and warm and
alive.

The fuzzy creature grew
bigger and bigger . . . .

. . . . until it filled both hands.

Fuzzy kept growing until
he filled both arms.

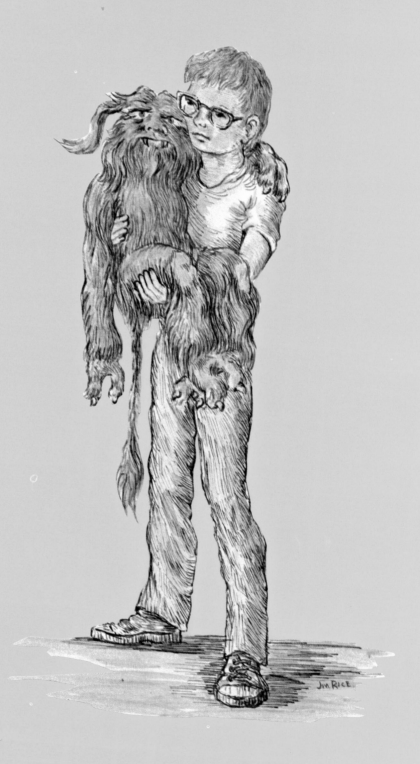

He grew as big as Lyn
and still he grew

—until he was a fully grown
Fuzzy, bigger than a horse.
No cowboy's horse could compare
with Fuzzy. His back was so
wide, so soft, so tall. Lyn and
Fuzzy were great friends.

They played games like no one
else could play, like loop
the loop and whirley bird.
They were the envy of
everyone.

Even plain everyday games
like pitch and catch were fun
with a friend like Fuzzy.
Fuzzy was so very strong that
a baseball thrown went up and
up and up and never
came down—
so it seemed.

Lyn and Fuzzy often walked
in the woods. One day a
cool breeze started to blow.
The breeze turned to wind and
blew and blew. Fuzzy grew
sad. He did not want to
play. Lyn thought Fuzzy
looked smaller and smaller
with each passing day. One day
Fuzzy was gone.

Lyn looked and called but
Fuzzy was gone,
and the cold wind blew.

It had been great having a friend
like Fuzzy but the great Fuzzy
comes but once to very special people
at a very special time and like
the fuzzy dandelion he is soon
gone.

Lyn went home, where it was
warm and the wind didn't blow.
Soon he was happy
again.

Somewhere a Fuzzy Seed
blows softly in the breeze. If
it stops where the sun is high
and warm and where someone
very young at heart waits with
a dream,
perhaps . . . .